SECRETS OF THE SNOW
VANISHING VOICES

ROSIE

Anne Wan

Illustrated by Dawn Larder

This paperback 2nd edition published in 2016 by

NORTH OAK PRESS

Text copyright Anne Wan, 2016
Illustrations by Dawn Larder, 2016
Illustration copyright Anne Wan, 2016

ISBN 978-0-9954864-1-6

A CPI catalogue record for this book is available from the British Library.

Printed and bound in the UK.

SECRETS OF THE
SNOW GLOBE
VANISHING VOICES

Anne Wan

Illustrated by Dawn Larder

Contents

For

Mum,

Daniel, Joshua and Joseph

xxx

.

Chapter 1
Magic At Work

Beyond the grey clouds, Louisa glimpsed a flicker of sunlight reflecting on a glass sky. Jack was right. They were trapped inside Grandma's snow globe and it was all her fault. She turned away from him, pained with guilt. If only she had not touched the globe…

* * *

She had not meant to touch it. She had been curled up on the sofa reading when she noticed a dazzling light shining from the glass dome. *How strange? It's never lit up before,* she puzzled.

She edged towards the display cabinet and opened the glass doors. She paused. *Grandma has told me not to touch it,* she reminded herself.

She recalled Grandma's warning. 'My father made it for me when I was a girl,' she had said. 'It's irreplaceable.'

'Can't we play with it if we're *very* careful?' her brother, Jack, had asked.

'No dear. It isn't a toy. Who knows what might happen if you touch it?'

Louisa hesitated. *What if Grandma or Grandad find me playing with the snow globe? Worse still, what if I drop it and break it?* She listened hard. Jack was chatting to Grandma in the kitchen. The distant hum of the lawn mower signalled that Grandad was still in the garden. She stared back at the shining globe. The urge to pick it up overwhelmed her. She

circled her fingers around the smooth sphere. 'Oh! It's ice cold!' she gasped. She lifted it from the shelf and perched on the sofa. Carefully, she lowered the globe onto her lap.

She rocked it gently. Inside, snow swirled around the mountain and miniature village. For the first time, she noticed that the brilliant light was shining from a fountain in the village square. Beside it, was the figure of an elderly gentleman. His forlorn expression caught Louisa's attention. *Why are you sad?* she mused.

She knew she must return the snow globe to the cabinet. *But I must hear the music first.* It was the music that made the snow globe so special. Louisa slid her fingers underneath the box and wound the oval key. The box was silent. 'Oh! It's broken!' she sighed.

Suddenly, she heard footsteps in the hallway. Louisa sprang to her feet. Before she could hide the globe, Jack burst into the lounge. His sharp, green eyes darted to the glowing sphere. 'You shouldn't be playing with that! Grandma will be cross!'

'I was just putting it back.'

'What's that strange light coming from it? I haven't seen that before,' he frowned.

'It's nothing,' she said, shielding it from him.

'I want to look. Let me have it,' he said. He reached for the snow globe.

Louisa clutched it tightly. 'I had it first. Leave it alone!'

'It's not yours! I want it!' cried Jack. He lunged at the orb.

Louisa swung it out of his reach. Jack missed and crashed to the floor. Undeterred, he leapt to his feet and dived towards her. Louisa fought to keep hold of the globe but it slipped from her fingers and spun into the air. Jack jostled against her, straining to be the first one to catch it. CRACK! The base split apart from the dome. THUD! It landed heavily on the carpet, narrowly missing Jack's foot. They looked up at the glass dome, hovering above them.

'Watch out!' cried Louisa, as snow poured from it like a waterfall. A sound like rushing water, filled the room. 'Jack!' she cried, as a gust of wind whipped the snow around them.

'Hold on to me!' he shouted.

'I can't see you!' she cried.

Icy snowflakes stung her cheeks and clung to her jumper. The wind spiralled into a tornado. It lifted them off the carpet and spun them round like clothes in a washing machine. 'My slippers!' cried Louisa, as they were flung from her feet and disappeared into the flurry of snow.

Just when she thought she might be sick, the wind stopped. They were suspended in mid-air.

'What's happening? I feel like I'm being squeezed!' wailed Jack.

Louisa watched in alarm as her arms and legs shrivelled towards her body. 'We're SHRINKING!' she cried.

'The base is pulling us down!' yelled Jack. 'We're being sucked into the globe!'

They tumbled towards the base, colliding with giant snowflakes as they fell. At last, they thumped into a snowdrift. A deep, 'CLUNK!' shook the ground as the glass dome slotted into place above them.

'What have you done?' hissed Jack, hauling himself out of the snow.

Louisa glanced round. Lining the square were rows of quaint, wooden shops, iced with a thick layer of snow. Women, wrapped in winter coats, shuffled from shop to shop carrying wicker baskets. At the far end of the square, a group of children were building a snow figure that looked like a grizzly bear.

Louisa struggled to her feet. 'I haven't done anything!' she said, pushing the tangled brown hair from her face. 'This is your fault. You shouldn't have snatched the snow globe from me!'

'We wouldn't be here at all if you hadn't taken the globe from Grandma's cabinet!'

snapped Jack, shaking the snow from his hair. He wrapped his arms around himself, trying to keep warm. 'What is this place?'

Louisa straightened up. Before her, a stone fountain jutted out of the snow. Louisa gaped at the streams of water that had frozen into ropes of ice.

'It's the fountain I saw in the snow globe,' she gasped. She lifted her gaze. Stretching beyond the village were the forest covered slopes of the mountain.

Her heart sunk. Her thoughts echoed Jack's, *what have I done?*

Chapter 2
I-Sing and Icicles

Louisa felt a tap on her shoulder. She turned to see an elderly gentleman. His coat hung loosely over his shoulders as he leant on a crooked stick. Wisps of grey hair poked out from underneath his pointed, fur hat.

'I know you,' said Louisa. 'I've seen you in the snow globe!'

His tufty eyebrows knotted into a frown.

'Do you speak English?' asked Jack.

The gentleman took a breath as if to answer then paused. His hand darted to cover his mouth. His wrinkled cheeks flushed crimson.

'He seems embarrassed. Why doesn't he talk?' whispered Louisa, shivering in the crisp air.

'Dunno. It looks like he's trying to tell us something.'

The man jabbed towards the sky then pointed at them.

'I think he wants to know how we fell from the sky,' said Louisa.

The gentleman smiled and nodded.

'We don't know,' she replied, brushing the damp snow from her leggings. 'We were playing with our Grandma's snow globe.'

'It split apart and snow poured out,' said Jack.

'We shrank and fell into your village,' Louisa finished.

The man's eyebrows arched in surprise. A look of concern crossed his face. He pointed at them and tilted his head.

'We're fine, thank you, just a bit dizzy,' said Louisa. 'What do you call this place?' She scanned the peculiar shops with shutters at the windows and curved roofs, dripping with icicles.

The scene reminded her of a postcard that Grandma and Grandad had sent from Switzerland.

The wizened man opened his mouth to speak then shook his head and sighed. He took a thin slate from his coat pocket. Using a stick of chalk he scrawled the word, 'I-Sing'.

'Icing?' said Louisa. 'That's odd.'

'The "Ice" bit's right!' whispered Jack, shivering.

The man wrote again in elegant, looping handwriting. 'I'm George. What are your names?'

'I'm Jack. This is my little sister, Louisa,' Jack replied.

Louisa frowned. She did not like being called *little*. After all, she was almost eight!

George smiled. He started to write again when a crowd of villagers moved closer.

Louisa began to feel uneasy. 'Jack, have you noticed how quiet it is? It doesn't feel right. No-one's talking!'

She stared at a little boy trying to talk to his Mum. He opened and closed his mouth but made no sound. *He looks like my goldfish,* thought Louisa, trying not to giggle.

Jack spoke to the crowd, 'Err.. hello. Can you help us? We need to get back to Grandma's house.'

The crowd stared blankly at him.

The silence made Louisa feel awkward. 'We've left her lounge in such a mess,' she added. 'She'll be so worried that we've disappeared.'

As she spoke, tears rolled down the cheeks of a little girl in a pale, blue cloak.

'Please don't cry for us,' said Louisa.

George waved his hands.

'I don't think we've upset her,' whispered Jack.

'Whatever's wrong?' asked Louisa.

The villagers scribbled on grey slates and held them for the children to see, 'Our voices! Stolen! It's The Miser...The Miser!'

'No voices? Stolen?' puzzled Jack.

'Who's The Miser?' added Louisa. 'He sounds scary!'

George leant forward and wrote, 'Selfish Man!' He pointed at the mountain peak beyond the village.

Louisa gazed at the snowy slopes that rose to a rocky point. *It's so bleak!*

George wrote, 'Too cold here. Come to my house. Tell you more.'

Louisa hesitated. She turned to Jack. 'We're not supposed to go with strangers,' she said, in a hushed voice.

'We'll freeze to death out here,' he replied. 'We've no choice. Come on.'

Chapter 3
A Dark Menace

They followed George as he shuffled across the square. The cold gnawed at Louisa's feet. She wished that she had not lost her slippers.

'Is it a long way?' she called.

George shook his head and smiled.

Louisa looked up at the vast sky. She almost believed that she was looking at *her* sky, *her* sun. But beyond the clouds, the sun's rays still danced on a sheen of glass. Louisa felt trapped. She sighed and carried on.

George led them through a small passageway between a dressmakers and a bakery. The sweet smell of fresh bread wafted over them. Jack lingered by the shop window.

'Come on,' said Louisa, tugging at his sleeve.

'I'm a bit peckish.'

'You're always peckish! We can't stop. Besides, we've no money. Even if we had we couldn't use it. Look! Their prices are in "Krones" or something not pounds!'

Jack stared at the labels. 'Humph,' he grunted and reluctantly dragged himself away.

As they followed George, Louisa heard the sound of snow crunching behind her. She glanced over her shoulder and saw the villagers following them. 'Why are they coming?' she whispered to Jack.

'Maybe they want to tell us about The Miser, too,' he shrugged.

At the end of the passageway, George opened a small door. He beamed with pride and ushered them into his front room. He lit a gas lamp and hung it from the ceiling.

'It's very cosy,' said Louisa.

George smiled and prodded the embers in the stone fireplace. He added extra logs. The fire crackled into life. As the villagers filed in, he beckoned Jack and Louisa to sit in the only armchair.

'Thank you,' said Louisa, grateful to be near the fire. She wriggled her toes, glad of the fur rug beneath her frozen feet.

Jack raised his hands towards the flickering flames. 'It's good to feel my fingers again!' he said.

'Me too!' said Louisa.

As she warmed her hands, she noticed an ornately carved bookcase beside the fireplace. *It's completely empty,* she thought. *How odd!* On top of the bookcase was a photograph of two boys. 'Is that you in the photo?' she asked George.

A twinge of sadness flashed across George's face. He nodded.

Louisa was about to ask who was the other boy, when the last villager squeezed into the room.

George took out his slate and began to write. He peered over his spectacles and held the slate for Jack to see.

'Last night, The Miser swept into our village,' Jack read aloud. He turned to the crowd. 'Is that so bad?'

The villagers gaped at him, gesturing wildly with their hands.

George scrawled on the slate once more then fixed his grey eyes on Jack. 'Swept, not walked! Magic!'

Jack began to squirm.

George lowered his whiskery chin and wrote, 'He broke into The Great Hall. Stole the crystal trumpet! Our most treasured possession!'

'That's mean!' said Jack.

George cleaned the slate and wrote again, 'Miser played trumpet. Didn't blow. Breathed in!'

'How strange!' said Louisa.

'Placed enchantment on trumpet. When we spoke, silver notes flew from our mouths!' wrote George.

Jack frowned.

'Wow! Like breath on a cold day?' said Louisa.

George pointed his chalk towards her as if to say, 'Spot on!' He wrote, 'Notes flowed into trumpet as Miser passed by. Our voices vanished!' He tapped his mouth and tried to speak. Despite his effort, he could not make a sound and looked foolish as he silently mouthed the words. His shoulders drooped. 'Exasperating!' he scrawled.

The villagers bobbed their heads in agreement.

'That's terrible!' said Jack.

'How frightening!' gasped Louisa. 'Jack,

imagine what it would be like to have no voice! How would we play with our friends? Or ask for help?'

Jack looked thoughtful. 'I tried a sponsored silence at school once. It was a nightmare! By morning break I thought I'd burst if I didn't say something! I didn't raise much sponsor money that day!' he grinned. 'I can't imagine not being able to talk forever. I'd go crazy!'

'Yes! I have to tell my friends everything. What if I was unable to talk to them at all!' said Louisa. 'I couldn't ask Grandad to help me train our new puppy and you couldn't ask Grandma for second helpings!'

Jack's face fell. 'This is serious!' He spoke to the villagers, 'What about food? Can you still eat?'

The crowd nodded.

'That's a relief!' he replied.

Louisa turned to George. 'It must be very frustrating having to write everything down.'

'It takes you ages!' said Jack. 'You must be really fed-up.'

The villagers nodded.

'I wonder how your teachers are managing?' mused Louisa.

'It's chaos!!!' wrote a slim man with a fraught expression.

'If our teachers lost their voices, they couldn't tell me off,' said Jack, looking smug. 'I'd like that!'

A woman holding the hand of a small boy, glared at him. She wrote, 'My son ran into street today. I tried shouting, "Stop!" but no use. Sleigh almost knocked him down!'

Jack's cheeks flushed red. 'Oh, I hadn't thought it might be dangerous! I'm sorry.'

The woman bobbed her head, accepting his apology.

A boy dressed in choir robes signalled to be given a slate. 'Tomorrow is I-Sing Music Festival,' he wrote. 'Without voices, festival is ruined! Can't sing!' He took a deep breath and lifted his chin. He opened his mouth but made no sound.

'You must be so disappointed,' said Louisa.

'Yes!' he wrote. 'Trained for weeks!'

The girl in the pale, blue cloak dripped tears on the slate as she wrote, 'Can't perform my solo. I've practised so hard!'

'What a shame,' said Louisa.

A stout man in the corner raised his

violin. Everyone watched as he skimmed his bow across the strings. The violin was silent.

'He's stolen your music too?' asked Louisa.

He nodded.

'Of course!' she cried. 'Jack, before you found me playing with the snow globe, I wound the music box but it was broken! The music wouldn't play. I couldn't understand why. Maybe it's because the villagers have had their music stolen!'

A man with a white beard and curly moustache wrote, 'We open festival by sounding trumpet. Dreadful it's stolen. Miser's spoilt everything!'

'Horrible man!' said Louisa. 'He's made your lives miserable, ruined your Music Festival and probably broken Grandma's snow globe, too!'

A lady motioned to George for the slate and chalk. Her hand trembled as she wrote, 'Worse than horrible! Monster!'

'What do you mean?' asked Jack, uneasily.

She wrote, 'Only glimpsed him at night. Moves in shadows. Doesn't like to be seen. Never know where he is or what he's doing!'

A ginger-haired boy snatched the slate and wrote, 'He wears hooded cloak to hide his face! Don't know what he looks like.'

'Maybe he's not even human!' wrote the choirboy.

'Where does he live?' Louisa asked anxiously, hoping it was far away.

'Vorgenhelm! Castle. Top of mountain,' wrote the violinist. 'Some say they've seen its turrets poking out of forest. No one's got close enough to be sure. Signs say "Keep Out!"'

A lady in a bright shawl wrote, 'Guarded by snow leopards. They never sleep. Prowl grounds night and day!'

Louisa's skin prickled.

'Hates to see us happy. Takes what we enjoy!' wrote George. 'Last year, he stole our books!'

'That's why your bookcase is empty!' said Louisa. 'Why is he so unkind?'

'Selfish!' wrote George. 'We call him "The Miser!"'

The villagers nodded.

'Why don't you go to Vorgenhelm Castle and get your voices back?' asked Jack.

The villagers' jaws dropped. Their eyes widen with fear. They shook their hands.

George wrote, 'When books stolen, men of I-Sing tried. Blizzards forced them to turn back. Always blizzards!'

'As if mountain or some force is working against us,' wrote the violinist. 'Too frightened to try again!'

'We'll get your voices back,' cried Jack. 'We'll find the trumpet and return it to the village. I like an adventure.'

Louisa was horrified. The villagers turned to one another in excitement.

'Are you mad?' Louisa hissed in Jack's ear. 'This is for real! You're not a hero in one of your comics now!'

Jack ignored her and spoke to the villagers, 'We're from a different world,' he said. 'Perhaps the mountain won't be able to stop us.'

George's face lit up. He threw his arms around Jack.

'This might be why the snow globe brought us to your village,' said Jack. 'We'll get the trumpet back from The Miser. You'll soon have your voices and music,' he beamed.

The villagers punched the air with delight.

'Jack, this is crazy,' whispered Louisa. 'Didn't you hear what they said about him?'

'Rumours,' Jack shrugged. 'Besides, Grandma always tells us to help others.'

'I want to go back to Grandma's house!'

'If the globe brought us here to help the villagers, it will send us back when we've returned the trumpet. Don't worry,' said Jack.

Louisa sighed. 'I hope you're right!'

Chapter 4
Hidden Treasure

George peered out of the window. 'It's nearly noon,' he wrote. 'You need to climb as far up the mountain as possible while there's daylight.'

The violinist pointed at their thin, damp clothes and shook his head.

'We haven't got anything else to wear,' said Jack, tugging at his striped, rugby shirt.

The little girl took off her pale, blue cloak and handed it to Louisa.

'For me?' said Louisa. 'Thank you!'

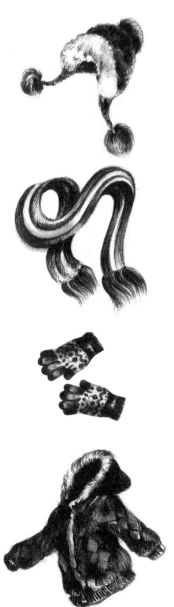

One by one, the villagers took off their jumpers, gloves, scarves and hats, and offered them to Louisa and Jack. 'I'll feel like a North Pole explorer in all these!' said Jack, staggering under an armful of clothes.

George rummaged in a cupboard under the window. He pulled out two pairs of furry boots for them.

The violinist signalled for the villagers to leave. He gave a message to Jack, 'See you at mountain path to say goodbye.'

Louisa watched the villagers bustle out of the

house. She wished that Jack had not volunteered to help. Climbing the mountain was going to be difficult. The idea of facing The Miser was terrifying! Why was Jack so reckless? He always blurted out ideas before thinking!

Louisa looked at the clothes she had been given. The whole village was relying on them to find The Miser and return their voices. She pictured the sobbing girl and the small boy who had almost been knocked down by a sleigh. *They need our help*, she thought. *We've got to try!*

Her thoughts were interrupted by George. 'I'll pack food,' he wrote.

'Can I help?' she asked.

He smiled and led her into a tiny kitchen. On the right, a black pot bubbled on a stove. George lifted the lid. The rich aroma of tomatoes and spices tickled Louisa's nose.

'Smells delicious!' she said.

George smiled.

Together, they poured the steaming soup into a large flask. They placed the flask, along with a loaf of bread and four spiced buns into a rucksack. George added a glass bottle of water and gave her the thumbs up.

'Thank you for the food,' she said, 'you've been so generous.'

George waved his hand as if to say, 'Don't mention it.' Then he paused and tapped the side of his nose with his finger. He gestured to Louisa to stand still. He bent down and reached into the cupboard.

What is he doing? she wondered.

Using the handle of a spoon, he levered open the back panel to reveal a secret compartment. Louisa gasped as he lifted out a velvet pouch and pressed it into her hand. Inside, she saw a glittering snowflake, twice the size of a fifty pence piece.

He took the slate from his pocket and wrote, 'Take this. It has magic powers. It will help you if you're in danger.'

'I can't take this,' murmured Louisa, nervous of being entrusted with such a precious keepsake.

'I trust you,' George wrote.

'Won't it break?' she whispered, turning the sparkling gem over in her hands.

He shook his head. 'Made of diamond!'

Louisa looked into his solemn eyes. 'Thank you. I'll look after it!' George smiled and wrote, 'I hope it will look after you!'

They returned to the lounge where Jack was surveying the pile of clothes. Louisa tightened her grip on the snowflake. *I can't let him see it,* she thought. *What if he tries to take it from me?*

She turned away and secretly slipped the snowflake into the pocket of the pale, blue cloak.

George handed the rucksack to Jack then took two, thick blankets from a wooden chest beside the front door.

'Why do we need blankets?' asked Jack.

George rested his head on his hands, pretending to go to sleep.

'For bed-time?' Jack questioned.

George nodded.

'I hadn't thought about spending the night on the mountain!' exclaimed Louisa. She shivered at the thought.

George wrote, 'Lama wool. Very warm! Only one night. You'll reach Vorgenhelm by midday tomorrow.'

'I hope we can find the castle,' Louisa worried.

'If I were younger, I'd come with you!' wrote George. 'You can do this!' His kind face creased into a smile.

Louisa felt hope rise within her.

'Do we need a map?' asked Jack.

George shook his head. He wrote, 'No-one else lives on mountain. I'll show you path through forest. It'll lead you to Castle.'

He tied the blankets onto the rucksack. Pulling on his fur coat, he urged them to hurry. They quickly dressed and followed him down the narrow passage.

The winding streets led uphill until they reached the edge of the village. A red-faced man, leading a dapple, grey horse, panted towards them. Seeing George, he tipped his tweed hat in respect. He turned to Jack and Louisa and waved his hands about.

'I'm sorry. We don't understand what you're trying to tell us,' said Jack.

The man looked frustrated. George gave him the slate and chalk. He beamed at once and wrote, 'You must be the young folk who are going to get our voices back!'

'Yep, that's us,' said Jack, puffing out his chest.

'This is Daisy,' the man wrote, pointing to the elegant horse beside him. 'She belongs to my daughter. She wants you to borrow her.'

'Really?' enthused Louisa. 'Please thank your daughter. Tell her I started riding lessons last summer. I know how to ride.'

'She looks a bit big!' said Jack, warily. 'I'm not fond of horses, especially when they're this tall.'

Louisa cast her eye over Daisy. She was definitely bigger than the ponies she was used to. She felt a flutter of nerves in her tummy. *I must try to be confident or Jack will never ride her,* she told herself. 'It'll be fun!' she said, brightly. 'Anyway, riding will be better than walking!'

She ruffled Daisy's silver mane and stroked her velvet nose.

The horse let out a low whinny and pressed her black muzzle into Louisa's hand.

'She's lovely,' Louisa breathed.

The owner pointed to Daisy's mouth then tapped a cloth bag, tied onto the saddle.

'Food for Daisy?' asked Louisa.

He gave the thumbs-up signal and handed her the reins. Louisa slid her foot into the stirrup and mounted the horse with ease.

'Erm…I might need some help,' said Jack, fidgeting awkwardly.

The man's shoulders shook as he gave a silent chuckle. With bear like arms, he took hold of Jack and swung him onto the saddle behind Louisa.

He scribbled a final message, 'She'll take good care of you. Safe journey!' He waved goodbye and returned to the village.

Louisa nudged Daisy with her heels. The horse set off at a brisk pace.

'Whoa!' cried Jack, as the motion threw him off balance.

'Hold onto me. You'll be fine,' encouraged Louisa.

As they rounded the corner, they saw a crowd had gathered to say goodbye.

George pointed at a parting between the trees. 'Path,' he wrote.

Louisa nodded.

George looked up at her and patted her hand.

'Goodbye. Thank you for all your help,' she said.

'Louisa, let's go!' cried Jack. 'Goodbye everyone!' he called, raising his hand grandly to the crowd like a knight, heading into battle.

Louisa's muscles tensed. *There's no going back now!*

Chapter 5
Chased By the Mountain

'I never thought I'd see you on a horse, Jack. You're doing really well!' said Louisa.

'Thanks! It's a bit uncomfortable,' he winced, rubbing his bottom.

Daisy's feet scrunched in the snow with a rhythmic beat. Louisa watched her tufty ears bob up and down. She ruffled the horse's silky coat. Daisy nickered softly.

'I think she likes you,' said Jack.

'I'm glad! We've got a long way to go together,' smiled Louisa.

The tall fir trees on either side of the path were so thick with snow that the branches drooped under the weight.

'I wish we had this much snow at home,' sighed Louisa. 'It would be great for building snowmen!'

'I'd like to sledge down this mountain! Think of how fast I'd go. Awesome!'

'You'd probably lose control and crash,' laughed Louisa. 'Remember the pile-up you caused last winter?'

'It's snowing again!' cried Jack, as white flakes began to drift from the metallic sky.

Louisa watched the delicate flakes twirl and dance as they meandered to the ground. 'It's strange how silent the flakes are when it snows,' she said.

'It's like magic!'

'It's too quiet. It makes me nervous,' said

Louisa, glancing left and right. 'What was that?' she asked, hearing the crack of twigs.

Jack scanned the forest and listened. A flash of brown flitted between the trees. 'It's a deer! Look! There's another one.'

They watched as two, slender deer stared back at them, their noses twitching.

'They won't hurt us,' said Jack.

Suddenly, the snow began to fall more swiftly.

'It's getting heavier!' cried Louisa.

Flakes no longer floated lazily but were driven to the ground by a harsh wind. Louisa and Jack bent forwards to protect their faces. Daisy dropped her head, bracing herself against the force of the storm.

'It's turning into a blizzard!' cried Jack.

'It's the power of the mountain!' wailed Louisa. 'It's why the villagers were forced to turn back!'

'Take cover in the trees.'

Louisa turned Daisy up the sloping bank to the left. The horse struggled and her hooves slipped. 'Come on!' Louisa urged.

As Daisy reached the shelter of the trees, Louisa heard a deep, rumbling sound echo across the mountainside. Daisy shuddered. She halted abruptly. Her muscles quivered. She tossed her head, snorting.

Jack gripped onto Louisa to keep his balance.

'There, there,' crooned Louisa, patting Daisy's neck.

But Daisy refused to calm down. She shook her head, neighed and stamped her hooves in the snow. The rumbling grew louder.

'It's coming from further up the mountain,' cried Louisa.

Trees trembled and clumps of snow slipped from the branches.

'The whole mountain's shaking!' shouted Jack. 'I think it's an avalanche!'

Louisa looked for an escape route. 'The trees are too close together. We can't get through the forest. We'll have to go back!' she cried. She turned Daisy towards the village and kicked hard, 'Yah!' she shouted against the wind. Daisy cantered down the slippery path.

'Ahhh!' wailed Jack. His grip tightened on Louisa as he bounced in the saddle.

Above the snow storm, they could hear the avalanche gaining on them. Louisa glimpsed over her shoulder. A towering wall of snow, mixed with uprooted trees and boulders, tumbled towards them.

'We can't outrun it!' shouted Jack.

Louisa remembered George's snowflake. She slid her hand into her pocket and clenched the diamond.

'Please help,' she breathed, and closed her eyes.

Just as the avalanche was about to swallow them, she heard the beating sound of great, powerful wings.

'Louisa! We're flying!' cried Jack.

She opened her eyes. The ground fell away beneath them as they rose above the tree-tops.

'Look at Daisy She's turned into a bird!' cried Jack.

Louisa glanced down at Daisy. She could still see the horse's familiar neck, head and tufty ears but stunning, white wings had sprouted from her shoulders.

'She's not a bird,' cried Louisa in delight, 'she's like Pegasus; a flying horse!'

She laughed as they turned and soared over the avalanche. They watched it thunder to a halt beneath them.

'We've beaten the mountain! Whoopeee!' cried Louisa, as Daisy flapped her magnificent wings and rose effortlessly above the forest. The cold wind rushed at their cheeks. Snowflakes peppered their faces.

'How has this happened?' cried Jack.

'It's magic!' shouted Louisa. Her tummy fluttered as Daisy tilted and swooped. 'This is better than any ride at the fair!'

'R-i-i-ght!' faltered Jack.

Louisa giggled. 'You're not so tough now are you, big brother?'

'I don't mind flying, I just don't like hei…ghts!'

Louisa squeezed on the right rein to guide Daisy further up the mountain. Below, they could see the devastation created by the avalanche. Great cascades of snow had crashed through the forest, bulldozing everything in its path.

'We could fly all the way to the top of the mountain!' cried Louisa.

'Do we have to?' wailed Jack.

'It would be much quicker.'

But suddenly, they began to lose height.

'What's the matter? We're going down!' called Jack.

'I don't understand,' Louisa replied. 'Daisy's flapping just as hard!' Then she noticed the horse's wings. They seemed smaller than before. 'It's Daisy's wings,' she cried. 'They're shrinking!'

The wings, once twice the size of Daisy,

were now less than a metre across. *The magic must be wearing off*, thought Louisa.

'Head for the path!' cried Jack.

Louisa squeezed the right rein to steer Daisy towards the path. The ground seemed to rush up at them at an alarming speed. Daisy flapped her stumpy wings until they shrank into her shoulders and disappeared. Thump! She landed with a jolt, catapulting Jack and Louisa into a bank of snow.

For a moment, no one moved. Louisa was the first to stir. She shook the snow from her cloak. Nearby, Daisy stood frozen to the spot, trembling with fright.

'It's alright, Daisy. Good girl,' Louisa soothed, edging towards her.

Daisy watched, wide-eyed. Slowly, Louisa reached out and caught the dangling reins. Daisy flinched.

'Poor girl,' said Louisa, patting her neck. 'That must have been quite a shock for you? It's not every day that you sprout wings and fly over an avalanche!'

'It was quite a shock for me too!' said Jack, standing up, caked in snow.

'Looks like we don't have to build a snowman after all,' giggled Louisa. 'We've already got one!'

'Ha-ha!' said Jack, sarcastically, brushing snow from his jacket.

Louisa looked at the gloomy sky. The snow had stopped falling. The howling wind had become a gentle whisper. Although the mountain had calmed down, Louisa felt a twinge of dread.

'Jack,' she gasped, 'have you noticed? It's getting dark!'

Chapter 6
Night Terror

Jack gazed at the mountain peak. 'We must be several miles from the top,' he said. 'George was right. We shan't make it to the castle before nightfall. We must find shelter.'

'Yes. Let's head into the woods. I can't see anywhere to shelter along the path,' said Louisa.

'We mustn't stray far. I don't want to get lost!' said Jack. 'Let's try here.' He ducked beneath the branches of two trees.

Louisa followed, leading Daisy. 'Come on,

girl,' she coaxed, tugging the reins. They emerged from the branches but Jack was nowhere to be seen. 'Jack? Where are you?' she called.

'Over here!'

His voice came from the far side of a small clearing. Louisa spied him, crouching at the base of a tree.

'This is good place,' he said, pointing at a hole inside the trunk.

Louisa knelt beside him. 'A hollow tree!' she cried.

'It's perfect!' Jack replied. 'The floor is dry and it'll protect us from the wind and snow.'

'Are there any spiders?' asked Louisa.

Jack scrambled into the hole. She could hear the sound of his glove scraping against the bark and the occasional thump.

'Not anymore!' he grinned, poking his head out of the opening.

'I still don't like the idea of sleeping in there,' said Louisa, peering inside the musty tree trunk. 'It feels creepy and smells like Grandad's mouldy compost heap!'

'You can't sleep outside!'

'I suppose. Is there room for both of us?'

'I think so. Anyway, I'm not going any further. I'm starving!' said Jack, glancing at his watch. 'Wow, it's gone six already. No wonder I'm hungry!'

Louisa looped Daisy's reins over a nearby branch and loosened the girth. She opened the bag of pony nuts and shook half onto the ground for Daisy to eat. 'That's all for now, girl. Better save the rest for morning.' She gave her a final pat and crawled next to Jack in the hollow.

He unpacked the flask and handed it to Louisa. 'You first.'

'Thanks, Jack!' said Louisa, surprised by his thoughtfulness. She drank the rich sauce. 'I hadn't realised how hungry I was,' she said, tearing a piece of bread from the loaf.

'I'm always hungry,' said Jack. 'I'm glad George packed hot food!'

Suddenly, Daisy gave an anxious whinny. She flicked up her head and stood tensely. Her eyes rolled.

'What's up, Daisy?' asked Jack.

'She's heard something. Horses can hear sounds several miles away,' said Louisa. She scrambled out of the hollow and stared at Daisy. The horse twisted her pointed ears like satellite dishes. Louisa listened too. In the distance, she heard a faint, mournful sound like a child crying.

Jack stood beside her. The cry became louder and changed to a gruff wail.

Louisa glanced nervously at Jack. 'It sounds like an animal,' she said. 'Look, over there!' She pointed at a brown shape, moving among the trees.

They watched in horror as a huge bear charged out of the forest, straight towards them! Daisy yanked against the branch where she was tied. The wood snapped. Terrified, she galloped out of the clearing.

'Daisy!' screamed Louisa.

'Leave her,' cried Jack, as the bear thudded closer. 'He'll want food!'

Petrified, Louisa was unable to move. Jack darted into the hollow and stuffed the bread and flask into the rucksack.

'We'll have to climb out of the bear's reach,' he cried, slinging the bag onto his back. He snatched Louisa's hand and pulled her towards the lowest branch.

'I've never climbed a tree,' wailed Louisa. 'I don't know how to!'

'I'll find the best places to hold. You follow. Let's go!'

Jack spoke with such force, that despite her fear, Louisa leapt after him. With swift motions, he scaled the tree trunk. Louisa followed, gripping the same knots and branches that he had used.

Across the clearing, the bear reared up on his powerful hind legs and punched the air with dagger-like claws. He let out a haunting yowl that echoed through the forest and exposed his jagged teeth.

Louisa's heart raced.

'Come on!' cried Jack, beckoning wildly from the branch above.

Louisa frantically searched for the next foothold to push herself further up the tree.

Below, she could hear the thud, thud of the bear as he galloped towards them with an easy stride. She strained to reach the next branch.

'Hurry!' shrieked Jack.

Louisa glimpsed the bear below. The tree shuddered as the beast landed his paws on the trunk and swung at Louisa's feet. His claws scraped against her boot. Her foot slipped. Her legs dangled helplessly. 'Argh!' she cried, desperately clinging onto the tree.

Jack reached down and gripped her wrist. 'Pull! Now!' he cried.

Louisa pulled as hard as she could. With their combined effort, Jack hoisted her to safety. She held onto Jack, panting for breath. Below, the bear swiped furiously at the air with dangerous paws.

'I thought bears were supposed to hibernate for the winter,' Louisa puffed.

'They are! Perhaps the avalanche woke him. He certainly got out of bed on the wrong side!' said Jack.

'Oh no!' cried Louisa, as she saw him dig his claws into the bark. 'Jack, he's climbing up!'

Chapter 7
Fixed

'The bread. Throw the bread for him!' cried Jack, rummaging in the rucksack for the loaf.

Together, they tore off chunks and tossed them to the bear. The hungry beast turned away from the trunk and thumped onto the forest floor. He rooted around for the bread hidden in the snow. When he had gobbled every piece, he stared back at the children.

'What else can we throw?' cried Jack.

Louisa pulled at one of the blankets tied

onto the rucksack. She shook it open and held the corners. As the bear returned to the foot of the tree, she released it. The blanket flopped onto the bear's snout. It covered his

eyes and wrapped around his head. He growled and pawed at it in confusion.

'That's great but he'll pull it off in no time!' cried Jack.

The snowflake, remembered Louisa. She reached into her pocket for the precious diamond. She held it tightly and whispered, 'We need help!'

Instantly, the bear threw back his head and yowled. Louisa watched in amazement as the blanket remained fixed onto his head. He grizzled and shook. He lurched and dived from side to side to get rid of it. Whatever he tried, he could not shake off the blanket!

At last, he gave up and lolloped back into the forest, letting out an angry growl as the blanket flapped about him.

Jack and Louisa giggled at the comical sight.

'Will the blanket stay on forever?' asked Jack.

'No. I'm sure it will wear off in the same way that Daisy's wings disappeared.'

'Wear off?' questioned Jack. 'Do you mean, magic?'

Louisa realised she had said too much. She focused on climbing down, purposefully ignoring the question. *Could she trust him? Would he try to take the snowflake and use the magic for himself?* She decided it was better not to tell him about the gem.

'What if the bear comes back?' she asked, trying to change the subject.

Jack dropped to the ground beside her. 'I'll build a fire. That'll keep the bear away. Keep us warm too!'

Louisa looked up at the darkening sky. The sun had almost set. 'What about poor

Daisy?' she said, looking anxiously through the trees.

'I'm sure she can outrun the bear!' said Jack.

'I hope so,' said Louisa. 'But I don't fancy the rest of the journey without her.'

'She'll be fine. I'm sure she can look after herself. She might even wander back to the village,' said Jack, gathering sticks and leaves. 'Did you know you can start a fire by rubbing sticks together?' he said.

'Or you could use these,' said Louisa, waving a box of matches.

'Where...?'

'They were in the rucksack. George must have packed them.'

'Good old George!'

Inside the cosy hollow, Louisa unrolled the blanket. 'I'm sorry I lost the other one.'

'It was clever of you to use it to confuse the bear!' said Jack, 'I suppose we can share.'

'I wonder if Grandma and Grandad will sleep tonight. And what about Mum and Dad? They must be so worried about us,' said Louisa, as they snuggled together in the hollow.

'Yes. We must get the trumpet tomorrow and return the villagers' voices. It's our only chance of getting back home,' said Jack.

'I'm frightened of meeting The Miser,' Louisa confessed. 'What if he takes our voices?'

'Afraid of him after you've fought off a grizzly bear? Pah! It'll be a piece of cake!' replied Jack. Then he added, 'You did good today.'

Louisa squeezed his arm and planted an affectionate kiss on his cheek.

'Ugh! That's disgusting!' he said, rubbing his face.

'Night, big brother!' Louisa grinned.

She closed her eyes and dreamt of flying horses and grizzly bears that looked just like Jack.

Chapter 8
An Unexpected Friend

Pale sunlight crept into the hollow. Louisa stirred. She felt caught in the dreaminess of sleep but was aware that her muscles were cold and stiff. She pulled the blanket up to her chin to keep out the chill breeze. As she did, she felt a puff of warm breath on her cheek. It smelt like cabbages. *Am I dreaming?* she wondered. Suddenly, a rough tongue licked her face.

The bear! She jolted awake, expecting to see the terrifying creature before her.

Instead, poking through the opening, was a slender, grey face.

'Daisy!' she exclaimed. 'Jack, wake up! It's Daisy!'

Jack groaned and squinted at the horse.

'You found us! Clever girl,' cried Louisa, rubbing Daisy's forelock and kissing her velvet nose. Daisy stepped away from the hollow. Louisa scrambled after her. She looked over the horse for injuries and checked the tack for damage. 'I think she's fine.'

'Good,' replied Jack, yawning. 'I didn't fancy walking the rest of the way!'

'I'm so relieved she's not hurt,' said Louisa, rubbing Daisy's neck.

She returned to the hollow where Jack still lay, curled up under the blanket. She frowned. 'Get up, lazybones!'

'What? It's not half seven yet!'

'We should eat and move on!'

'Alright. On my way,' said Jack, lying motionless with his eyes closed.

Louisa scowled. She made a snowball and threw it at him. Domph!

'Hey! Okay! I'm coming!'

'I hope so, or I'll eat your spiced bun!'

They huddled around the glowing remains of the fire.

'We'd better save two buns for later,' said Louisa. 'We haven't got much food left.'

Jack nodded. 'I hope we find the trumpet and return the music and voices to the villagers today,' he said, with his mouth full. 'If we succeed, the snow globe might send us back to Grandma's house tonight! This time tomorrow we could be tucking into some of her tasty pancakes!'

'I bet Grandma and Grandad are so anxious about us. What must Mum and Dad be thinking too?'

'Well, I'm not looking forward to facing Grandma and explaining why we left her living room knee-deep in snow!' said Jack.

'Yes!' said Louisa. She stopped eating and turned the bun over in her hands. 'Jack, I've been wondering, what do we do when we've got the trumpet? I mean, how do we make it give the voices back?'

'Mmm. If The Miser breathed in through the trumpet when he stole the voices, I guess they'll come out if we blow it!'

Louisa agreed. She lifted her gaze to the top of the jagged mountain. 'This climb is not going to be easy!'

They finished breakfast and mounted Daisy. She set off with energetic steps.

Before long, the snowy track became narrow as it twisted higher. It felt as if the trees either side were closing in on them.

'I hope the trees don't block the path completely. We'll get lost if we can't follow the track,' said Louisa.

'George said this route will lead us to the castle. We have to trust that he's right,' replied Jack.

'It's so quiet. It gives me the creeps,' said Louisa, looking over her shoulder.

'You said that yesterday,' laughed Jack.

As his laughter faded, a strange hush fell over the woods. The only sound was the scrunch of Daisy's hooves in the snow. A mist appeared through the trees. Soft as a whisper, it drifted across the path. It crept around Daisy's legs and floated upwards. Gradually, the eerie vapour became a thick fog. Louisa could no longer see beyond Daisy's ears. Even her own hands were blurred as she held the reins. 'I hope Daisy can see where she's going, Jack. I can't see anything!'

'She's good at sensing danger. She'll keep us out of trouble,' he said.

Daisy began to puff with the effort of climbing as the path became steeper.

'Daisy's struggling. She'll find it easier if we lean forwards,' said Louisa.

They leant onto Daisy's mane. As they climbed higher, Louisa noticed that the fog was thinner on their right. She glanced down. The edge of the narrow path was only inches away from Daisy's hooves!

She gasped. 'Jack, look!'

Beyond the path was a sheer drop down a steep rock face! A ball of snow flicked from Daisy's hoof and bounced down the precipice. It smashed on the rocks then vanished into the abyss.

'What kind of path is this?' gulped Jack. 'If Daisy slips, we'd never survive the fall!'

'Hold tight. Try not to move. We mustn't unbalance her.'

Louisa felt Jack's arms grip around her waist. Her heart thumped as she clutched the front of the saddle. They sat as still as they could, hardly daring to breathe.

Chapter 9
Crack!

Louisa's hands ached from clenching the saddle. Her back was stiff. *I can't lean forward much longer,* she thought, when suddenly, the fog began to lift. As the mountainside became clear, Louisa realised that the path had turned away from the cliff altogether. 'Jack, we're out of danger!' she cried. 'Well done, Daisy!'

'I knew she'd keep us safe,' said Jack.

'Rubbish! You were as scared as I was. You squeezed me so hard I thought I'd pop!'

Jack drew breath to answer when he a saw

a wooden sign at the side of the path. 'Someone doesn't want visitors!' he said.

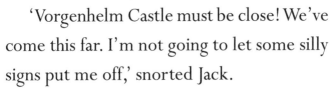

'There's another sign,' cried Louisa, pointing further along the track. 'Oh! "Turn Back Now! Or Else!" What should we do?'

'Vorgenhelm Castle must be close! We've come this far. I'm not going to let some silly signs put me off,' snorted Jack.

Just then, a shrill screech caused them both to look up. Overhead, circled a flock of black, menacing birds.

'What are they?' cried Louisa, shuddering at the sight of their poised talons and hooked beaks. 'They're enormous! Like vultures!'

The creatures gave piercing squawks and swooped towards them. Louisa buried her head in Daisy's mane.

'Clear off!' bellowed Jack, waving his arms madly.

Undaunted, the birds continued their descent. They were almost upon them when suddenly, Daisy reared up. She beat the air with her front hooves. Louisa was tossed backwards. She clung onto Daisy's mane.

'Whoa!' cried Jack, grabbing Louisa.

The birds lurched sideways to avoid Daisy's thrashing, metal shoes. The horse thudded to the ground and swung round to face the startled creatures. She shook her head and let out an angry neigh like a war cry. Terrified, the birds scattered. They cawed woefully and disappeared into the clouds.

'Wuh-hoo!' cried Jack. 'Good job, Daisy!'

'Have they all gone?' asked Louisa.

'Yes. Daisy's frightened them off! Let's hurry in case they return.'

Louisa glanced warily at the sky. She nudged Daisy forward. 'Is it much further do you think?' she asked, as they followed the winding path.

'No. Look!' cried Jack, pointing to a grey turret peeping out through the tree-tops. 'We must be getting close!'

Before long, the trees parted and Daisy halted. A carpet of unspoilt snow stretched out before them in a circle. In the centre, towered the vast walls of Vorgenhelm Castle. The grey stone looked dirty and drab against the white background of snow. The parapets were crumbling and stones were missing.

Louisa frowned. 'It's falling down! The battlements are like an ugly row of teeth.'

'Yeah, like mine,' grinned Jack, showing the gaps where his baby teeth had fallen out.

'Do you think The Miser lives here? It looks deserted,' said Louisa.

'I hope he's here. Otherwise we've travelled all this way for nothing!'

'I don't like it. Those narrow windows look like angry faces. It's as if the castle is glaring at us!'

'I can't wait to explore inside. It'll be great! I bet there are secret passages and tunnels!' said Jack.

'You've read too many books! Oh no! It's the birds again!' cried Louisa. Her heart pounded as the flock of vultures hovered over the grim castle. The largest bird left the others and dived towards the building, disappearing from view. The rest of the flock flew away.

'Did you see that? The vulture flew inside the castle!' said Jack.

'Yes! I'm glad the rest have gone.'

'Let's get closer.'

Louisa nudged Daisy forwards but the horse tossed her head and stepped backwards.

'Come on, girl,' Louisa encouraged. She prodded Daisy more firmly with her heels but the horse refused to budge. 'The last time she did this it was because she sensed the avalanche. What could be bothering her now?' Louisa puzzled. 'We should dismount.'

They slid from the saddle.

'Let me try,' said Jack, and took the reins. He tugged them gently, but Daisy snorted and pulled away.

'There's nothing to be afraid of Daisy,' he said.

'I'll show you,' called Louisa. She trudged ahead through the snow. After walking several metres, she turned. 'See, Daisy? It's quite safe.'

Suddenly, a deep cracking sound splintered beneath her feet. She froze.

'What's up? Is everything okay?' called Jack.

Louisa held her breath. Slowly, she scraped the snow aside with her foot.

Beneath her was a crackled sheet of ice. 'Oh no!' she cried, 'I'm on a lake!'

Without warning, the cracks streaked through the ice like shafts of lightening. She glanced up at Jack. Too late. Snap! Splash! The ice gave way. She plunged into the biting cold water.

Her arms flailed through the icy depths as she fought against the weight of her clothes. The water gurgled in her ears, muffling Jack's shrieks. She strained towards the patch of light in the broken ice. Jack's arm appeared in the water. She stretched her hands towards him but sank further and further away.

Chapter 10
Sinking

Her lungs screamed for air. Her head spun from the chilling cold. Her vision blurred. She felt herself drifting from consciousness when something shone in the water. The snowflake! She pulled off her mitten and caught the shimmering diamond.

Please, she begged as her eyes closed. The world began to fade.

Suddenly, she felt Jack's hand seize her wrist and pull her towards the surface. Cold air slapped against her cheeks as she emerged. Jack dragged her off the ice and turned her onto her side. He thumped her back until she coughed up the water. 'Louisa, I thought you had drowned,' he cried, shakily.

Louisa filled her lungs with great gulps of air. She blinked and gazed up at his anxious face. 'I'm alive!' she gasped.

'How did I manage to grab you?' said Jack. 'I thought I'd lost you. I saw you sink out of reach. Next, I found myself pulling you out! I don't understand?'

Louisa opened her quivering hand and showed him the diamond snowflake. Jack's jaw dropped.

'It has m-magic powers,' she said, shivering. 'G-George gave it to me to help us in times of t-trouble.'

'That explains a lot! Does it do anything you want?' Jack asked, staring at the gem.

'I don't think so. It's only w-worked when we've been in d-danger.'

'You'd certainly have drowned without it!' said Jack, holding her tightly.

'S-s-steady,' Louisa stuttered through chattering teeth, 'everyone will th-think that you care about your li-tt-tt-le sis-t-ter!'

Jack looked down at her with fresh alarm. 'Your lips are turning blue! You need to get dry or you'll freeze!' He swiftly took off her wet clothes. He wrapped the blanket around her.

She tried to move her arms but they felt like lumps of stone. Her eye-lids drooped heavily. *I must stay awake!* she thought.

In front of her, she could just make out Jack stripping off layers of jumpers.

'Why are you w-wearing s-so many c-clothes?' she stammered.

Jack grinned, 'The villagers kept giving me more and more. I didn't want to seem ungrateful. It didn't occur to me to say that I had enough! Good job too. I can share them with you. You'll be warm in no time!'

Jack dressed her in the dry clothes. Louisa tried to smile but the cold had sunk deep into her body. She shook uncontrollably.

'I'll light a fire,' he said, with forced calmness. He darted among the trees, gathering wood. With trembling hands, he lit the fire close to her. He heated the flask containing the remains of the soup. After cooling the rim, he held it for Louisa to drink.

The warm liquid felt like a stream of lava as she swallowed. The warmth radiated throughout her body. Gradually, she felt her strength return.

'Thank you,' she murmured.

Jack's anxious face relaxed. 'It's good to see you looking better! Daisy's pleased too!'

The horse grunted and padded towards them. She rubbed her soft nose against Louisa's cheek.

'That tickles,' giggled Louisa, as Daisy's whiskers brushed against her skin. 'I'm glad to see you too!'

Daisy snorted and rested her chin on Louisa's shoulder.

'I still don't understand what happened,' said Louisa, 'did I walk onto a lake?'

Jack glanced at the stretch of snow that encircled the castle. 'No. Not a lake. I think Vorgenhelm is surrounded by a moat!'

Chapter 11
A Dangerous Crossing

'How can we cross a moat?' asked Louisa. 'There's no bridge. The ice is too thin to walk on!'

Jack didn't answer. He was staring at the castle. Then he turned to a huge tree behind them. 'I've got an idea. Here, we're standing on firm ground. Right? See those snowy humps by the castle wall?'

'Yes.'

'I think those are bushes. That means the ground is solid over there.'

'How does that help us to cross?'

'I'll show you!' He untied the rope from the blanket. He slung it over his shoulder and began to climb the tree. It was unlike the trees which Louisa had seen on the mountainside. Its trunk was thick and knobbly. Majestic branches sprouted out in every direction like the tentacles of a giant octopus.

'This tree is easy to climb!' called Jack, pausing halfway to the top to wave at Louisa.

'Be careful!'

Jack gave her the 'thumbs-up'. He swivelled onto a branch that stretched across the moat, towards the castle. With his tummy scraping against the bark, he inched towards the tip. While hovering dangerously over the moat, he carefully removed the rope from his shoulder. One mistake and he would fall.

Louisa watched as he wound the rope around the branch and tied it in a triple knot. Cautiously, he edged back towards the trunk. She sighed with relief as he scrambled safely to her side.

'So what's your plan?' she asked, hoping that she wouldn't have to climb the tree.

'You're going to hold this,' said Jack, showing her the loose end of the rope, 'and swing across the moat. When you're close to the bushes on the far side, let go. You should land on firm ground!'

'It's a good idea but I'm afraid of falling through the ice again.'

'I know you are. I'll go first and test it. You'll see that there is nothing to be afraid of!'

Daisy sensed that they were about to leave. She hung her head and whimpered.

'You can't come with us, old girl. You'll be alright here,' said Jack.

'I don't want to leave you, Daisy, but we have to,' said Louisa. She rubbed the horse's forehead. 'We'll come back. I promise.'

Jack tugged the rope to make sure the knot was tight. 'The branch will hold my weight,' he said.

He shuffled backwards as far as the length of rope would allow and climbed onto an old tree stump for extra height. 'Piece of cake,' he said.

Clutching the rope in both hands, he leapt. Like a trapeze artist in the circus, he swung towards the castle at great speed. As he neared the far side, he let go of the rope. But the momentum was too great. Instead of dropping to the ground, he was flung towards the castle wall!

'Jack!' screamed Louisa. She shut her eyes, expecting to hear a sickening thump. She waited. Silence. She looked up. The trailing rope swung limply towards her. Forgetting her fear, she grabbed hold of it and launched herself across the moat.

The wind whistled past her ears as she whooshed towards the castle. As she neared the bushes, she let go of the rope and tumbled into the snow.

'Jack!' she yelled, staggering to her feet.

'I'm okay!' his voice echoed.

Louisa looked up. Jack's beaming face poked out of a window, a metre or so above her.

'Good job the glass was missing in this frame,' he grinned.

'I thought you were going to crash into the wall! I was worried you'd hurt yourself!'

'Here,' he said, offering his hand to Louisa.

She took it and climbed up through the empty window.

'It smells rotten in here!' she said. She eyed the green slime that clung to the walls. 'Urgh! Spiders' webs too!' She flinched at the wispy cobwebs that hung like bunting from the ceiling. Crates of rubbish, and old furniture littered the room. 'It's messier than your bedroom, Jack!'

'Yeah, I thought I was untidy!'

'The Miser doesn't seem to care about his castle. Look! Rat droppings,' she cried, pointing to black pellets, scattered across the stone slabs.

'That's disgusting!' said Jack. 'Let's get out of here! Mind where you tread!'

They picked their way carefully to the door. As they did, Louisa paused. 'Did you hear that?' she said.

They stood still, listening intently.

'It's music,' said Jack. 'It must be the crystal trumpet!'

Louisa swallowed hard. 'We're close to The Miser!'

Chapter 12
Face to Face

They stepped into a courtyard, lit by flaming torches.

'This place is deserted,' said Jack. 'I thought The Miser would have servants.'

'Who would want to live here?' shrugged Louisa.

Jack nodded.

'Do you hear that? It sounds like a violin!' Louisa said.

'The trumpet must be playing the violinist's music!' replied Jack.

Louisa's heart raced. 'Jack, what if The Miser takes our voices or worse?'

'We've got this far, haven't we? Have you got the snowflake ready?'

Louisa patted her pocket. 'How are we going to convince him to give us the trumpet?'

'I don't know. We'll work it out when we meet him.'

'The music is coming from over there,' said Louisa. She pointed to an arched door on the opposite side of the courtyard. They heard a different piece of music begin to play. The sound of the violin changed to the thumping beat of a brass band.

Jack signalled to move. As they tiptoed across the courtyard, they were startled by a squawk over-head.

'The vulture!' cried Louisa.

The bird swooped down. He landed on a ledge above the door and glared at them.

'He's guarding the entrance.'

'Quick!' said Jack.

They dived towards the door and slipped through. Jack spun round and shoved the door shut before the vulture could follow. Outside, they could hear him cawing in anger. They leant against the door to catch their breath.

They found themselves standing in a vast hall. It looked as though it had once been grand. Now, the walls were cracked and the paintings were faded. Candles lit the room with an eerie light and cast shadows into every corner.

'The villagers' books!' breathed Jack, gaping at a bookcase the size of a double-decker bus.

'Look! There's the trumpet!' whispered Louisa, pointing to the far end of the hall where the instrument was displayed on a golden stand.

Before Jack could respond, a croaky voice cried out, 'I-is someone there? Come forward and show yourself!'

They glanced at the opposite side of the hall. For the first time, they saw him: The Miser!

He sat, hunched on an over-sized chair with a cream spotted rug at his feet. His black cloak draped over his shoulders and cascaded onto the floor. He gripped a wooden staff with gnarled fingers. They could not see his face except for a crooked nose that poked out from under his hood like a beak.

'He looks like the black vultures!' whispered Louisa.

'Yeah. But a lot more miserable!' replied Jack.

The Miser leant forward. 'I hear intruders,' he muttered. 'Who are you? Show yourselves!'

They stepped into the light.

He raised his head in surprise. 'Children? *You,* breached my avalanche?' he said, incredulously. 'C-can't you read the signs? I hate visitors!' He banged his staff on the ground.

Louisa shuddered.

'How dare you invade my castle?'

'You've stolen the villagers' voices!' cried Jack. 'It's caused chaos! Yesterday, a boy was almost knocked down by a sleigh!'

The Miser jerked backwards. 'You can speak?'

'Yes!' smirked Jack, 'You didn't steal our voices!'

Louisa looked at her brother with admiration. Courage rose within her. 'We're here to help the villagers! You've stolen their music too! You've ruined their Music Festival. You've made everyone miserable! We've come to return the trumpet to the village and give everyone their voices and music back. They don't belong to you!'

The Miser chuckled. Then he roared, 'Ha, ha, ha. You? Take the trumpet? Return the voices and music?' he croaked. 'Ridiculous! You're just puny children!'

He lowered his chin. His voice became stern, 'I'm keeping their voices and music. The trumpet's mine! No one else can have it! You'll see.'

He patted his knee and whistled. At once, the spotted rug leapt up on all fours.

'I thought that was a rug!' said Louisa.

'Me too! It's a snow leopard!' cried Jack.

'We have unwelcome visitors, Ice-Claw. See them off!' cried The Miser.

The great snow leopard turned from his master like an obedient dog. He glowered at them with piercing blue eyes. A menacing growl rumbled in his throat as he prepared to attack. Suddenly, he bolted towards them.

'Stand still, Louisa. He's trying to frighten us!'

'It's working!' she yelled.

'Hold your ground!' cried Jack.

The creature's sharp claws scraped on the stone slabs as he drew close.

Jack grabbed Louisa's hand. 'Keep hold of the snowflake. Duck when I say!'

The snow leopard was almost upon them. He tucked his hind legs beneath him and leapt.

'Now!' cried Jack. He pulled Louisa to the ground.

The leopard soared over their heads and skidded to a halt. He whirled round to confront them. Louisa and Jack jumped to their feet. The beast snarled, revealing his carnivorous teeth.

Jack began to back off when Louisa boldly

stepped forward. She wagged her finger angrily. 'Naughty kitty!' she scolded. 'Lie down and stay!'

To Jack's amazement, the animal gave a pitiful whimper. He dropped his head in submission and tucked his tail between his legs. Louisa grinned triumphantly as the leopard stepped away from them and lay down. She patted the snowflake in her pocket and winked at Jack. 'I was told to trust it, remember?'

'W-What!?' fumed The Miser. 'Ice-Claw, chase them!'

The snow leopard twitched his tail and began to snore!

'I won't be beaten by two children!' The Miser seethed.

He placed one hand on his chest. Instantly, a rope appeared from nowhere and bound itself around Louisa and Jack. Louisa wrestled against the ropes to be free. The Miser waved his bony hand. They were lifted off their feet, wriggling like fish caught in a net.

'Ha, ha, ha. You can't outsmart me, you little imps!'

'You've taken the villagers' voices,' gasped Jack, 'but it isn't making you happy! You look completely miserable!'

The Miser tightened his grip on his staff and scowled at them. He raised a crooked finger and rotated it in a slow, circular motion. As he did, Jack and Louisa began to spin round.

'Arrgggh!' cried Jack.

Louisa's head reeled.

'The snowflake,' Jack hissed.

Louisa fumbled to free her hand from the

ropes and reach into her pocket. As soon as she touched the magical gem, the ropes fell away and they dropped onto the floor.

The Miser gasped in surprise, 'What? How did you…?'

'You can't scare us with your magic tricks!' exclaimed Jack, staggering to his feet.

'Really?' sneered The Miser. 'I don't like snooping children breaking into my home. Trying to steal from me!'

'That's exactly what you've done to the people in the village!' returned Louisa.

The Miser looked like a boiling volcano ready to explode. 'I want…' he snarled, but could say no more. He tried to speak but the words seemed to stick in his throat. He took a deep breath, 'I want…their voices and music! They're mine…mine…mine!' he cried, shaking his fist.

'He's like a spoilt child!' said Louisa.

'What are you s-saying?' spat The Miser. 'Enough of this! I'll take your voices too!' He rose to his feet.

'Quick!' shouted Jack. 'Let's grab the trumpet before he does!'

They sprinted towards the golden stand. The Miser raised an arm towards them and let out a rasping cry. A thick wall of glass shot up from the floor in front of them.

They skidded to a halt. Jack lurched to the left to advance around it. Up sprang a second sheet of glass. Behind them they heard, swoosh, swoosh as two more panes appeared. They were trapped inside a glass prison!

'He-hey,' The Miser chuckled. He shuffled towards his captives. 'You can't get the better of me,' he sneered.

Louisa and Jack slid their hands over the glass panels. They pushed against the enclosure and banged it with their fists.

'There's no escape,' said Jack. 'Use the snowflake.'

Louisa looked at him in dismay. She held out her hand and unfurled her fingers to reveal the gem.

'I am trying. Nothing is happening!'

The Miser closed in on them.

'It's not using magic to help us because it doesn't need to. It's a diamond!' exclaimed Jack. 'It can cut through glass!' He took the snowflake from Louisa's palm and dragged it across the wall.

Louisa pressed her hands over her ears to block out the screech. A crack appeared in the glass. Jack gave the cut pane a gentle push. It crashed to the floor.

'We're free!' he cried, and tugged Louisa towards the opening. Broken glass scrunched under their feet as they ducked through the hole. They straightened up, only to find themselves face-to-face with The Miser!

Chapter 13
Secrets Revealed

The Miser stepped closer. 'You don't look like children from the village. They're paler.'

'We're not from the village,' said Jack, drawing himself up as tall as he could.

The Miser's eyes drifted from Jack's face to his clenched fist. His angry frown softened. 'What's that in your hand, boy?' he puzzled.

Jack held the snowflake tightly against his chest. 'It's nothing!' he said, defensively.

'It's a diamond. A snowflake, isn't it? I saw

you use it to cut the glass.'

Jack shot an anxious glance at Louisa. 'You can't have it,' he cried.

The Miser stepped nearer. Louisa was surprised that he was only a little taller than Jack. He seemed so frail now that she could see him clearly. She almost felt sorry for him.

'It was given to us by a friend,' she said.

The Miser raised his eyebrows in surprise. 'Who was it? Could it have been…G-George?'

Louisa gasped. 'How do you know it was George?' she asked, incredulously.

'Because…' His face became solemn. He shook his head and shuffled away. 'Leave me alone!' he snapped.

'Please,' implored Louisa, taking hold of his sleeve. 'He's our friend. Tell us how you know him.'

The Miser let out a heavy sigh. 'I know him because…because he's my brother!'

'Your brother!' chorused Jack and Louisa.

'You're the other boy in the photograph,' said Louisa, recalling the picture on George's bookcase.

The Miser slid back his hood so they could see his face clearly. Without it, he appeared less like a bird and more like their friend, George.

'You do look alike! You have the same grey eyes!' Louisa exclaimed.

'And I have something else,' said The Miser. He peeled back his cloak to reveal a long chain hanging around his neck. On the chain, were nine, dazzling, diamond snowflakes!

Louisa stared at them. They were identical to the one that George had given to her!

'That's where your magic powers come from,' exclaimed Jack. 'Does George know that you're his brother?'

'No. He doesn't know who I am.' The Miser hung his head, ashamed.

'Everyone in the village calls you, "The Miser",' said Jack.

The Miser shrugged. 'I suppose I d-d-deserve that name. They must think I'm very selfish.'

'What's your real name?' asked Louisa.

'My name is Harry. I've hidden from the villagers for...oh... more than s-sixty years!'

'So long?' cried Jack.

The Miser nodded. 'I didn't want anyone to·know who I was. I w-wanted to be left alone. That's why I scare people away.'

He returned to his chair. Come, I'll explain,' he said. As he spoke, he patted a snowflake that hung around his neck. At once, the music quietened to a lullaby. As it softened, the cawing of the vulture could be heard.

'My poor pet! Are you shut out?' He held another snowflake on his chain. The door opened and in flew the impatient creature. He perched on Harry's shoulder and fixed his watchful eyes on Louisa and Jack.

'Ah, my beauty. That's better,' said Harry, stroking the bird's sleek feathers. He sank into his wooden chair and waved his hand. Two more chairs appeared for Jack and Louisa.

'Please, sit down,' he said, 'and I'll tell you my story. It begins years ago when George and I were about your age. We found

a clearing of fresh snow in the f-forest. We made a snowman. When the sun shone, we noticed that it glittered in a strange way. We looked closer and saw several d-diamond snowflakes pressed into the snow.'

'How did they get there?' asked Jack.

'We didn't know. They must have been mixed with the snow in the clearing.'

'Did you realise that they had magical powers?' asked Louisa.

'Not at first. We demolished the snowman and searched the area for more. We found t-ten in total. We shared them between us.'

'That sounds fair,' said Jack.

'It was. But I was not content with five snowflakes. I wanted them all! That night I crept into George's room and took them.'

'That's stealing! You must have known it was wrong,' said Louisa.

'Yes. I knew I shouldn't have taken them. I fled the village and followed the path up the mountain. I realised that George would find out in the morning that I'd taken the snowflakes. I felt guilty and couldn't bear to f-face him. I hid in the forest.'

'How did you discover that the snowflakes had magic powers?' asked Jack.

'I tried to build a shelter from branches.

It was flimsy and draughty. Frozen, I slid my hands into my pockets. I longed for a warm cabin. My hand brushed against one of the snowflakes. At once, a wooden cabin appeared!'

'How exciting!' cried Jack.

'It was!' Harry enthused. 'Once I'd discovered the snowflakes had magic powers, I didn't need to go back to the v-village. I used the magic to reach the top of the mountain and build this castle, far away from everyone.'

'Why did you have only nine snowflakes?' asked Jack.

'When I reached the mountain top, I realised that one was missing. I thought it had fallen from my pocket on the journey. I searched and searched for it. I must have dropped it in George's bedroom.'

'Don't you care that you've stolen from your brother and abandoned him?' said Louisa.

Harry gazed at his feet. 'It happened a l-long time ago,' he mumbled.

'Isn't it lonely here, by yourself?' asked Jack.

Harry shrugged, 'I've forgotten what it's like to be with people. I never had friends. George was the popular one. Everyone used to laugh at me and tease me.'

'Why?' asked Louisa.

Colour rose in Harry's cheeks. His voice trembled as he tried to speak, 'I struggled to…to…' He turned aside, blinking away tears.

'It's alright,' said Jack. 'You can tell us.'

Harry swallowed hard and looked back at them. 'I suppose it doesn't matter now,' he said. 'People teased me because I c-could barely speak. I stuttered badly, you see.'

'You hardly stutter now. You managed to shout at us easily enough!' said Jack.

Harry tapped the worn cover of a book that lay on the arm of his chair. 'I found this book among those I took from the village,' he said.

Louisa read the title, 'Fluency for Stammering.' She frowned. 'What does that mean?'

'It teaches techniques to help people speak clearly.'

'That's why you don't stutter anymore?' Louisa asked.

Harry nodded. 'It's been hard. Hours of practice! I talk to my pets. I'm comfortable chatting to them.'

'Why did you take the villagers' voices?'

'Humph!' Harry snorted. 'They're always so happy! I was fed-up with their laughing and chatting!'

'So you do visit the village!' cried Jack.

Harry grunted. 'It's so easy for them!' he snarled. 'Now they know what it feels like to be unable to speak!'

'That's spiteful!' cried Louisa.

'People were spiteful to me!'

'You've made the villagers' lives miserable! It hasn't made you happy, has it?' said Louisa.

'I want to be happy. That's why I took the music!'

'I don't understand?' said Louisa.

'I saw how much the villagers enjoyed playing their instruments and singing as they prepared for the festival,' he explained.

'You'd enjoy the music more if you shared it instead of keeping it for yourself,' said Louisa.

Harry gazed at the crystal trumpet. 'What do you want me to do?' he asked. 'Just give you the trumpet?'

Louisa looked hopefully at Jack. 'I've got a better idea!' she said. 'Why don't you come to the village with us? You can return the voices and music yourself! With your magic, they could continue with the Music Festival tonight. You might even enjoy helping them!'

Harry grimaced at the idea. 'They hate me!'

'You must come! Perhaps we can make the villagers understand how they've hurt you,' said Louisa, gently taking his frail hand.

He drew back slightly, surprised by her kind gesture.

'You can show the villagers that you're sorry too,' she said.

'You'll see George again,' added Jack. 'Don't you want to see him? I'm sure he'd be pleased to see you!'

Harry looked doubtful.

'We could take the trumpet and leave you to be miserable!' goaded Jack.

'Oh, alright!' Harry sighed. His eyes were drawn to the enormous bookcase. 'I suppose I should return the villagers' books too?'

'Definitely!' chorused the children.

Harry huffed and shuffled over to the bookcase. He slid a slim, gold box from the shelf.

'What's he up to?' whispered Louisa.

Jack shrugged.

Harry opened the box and blew onto the bookcase. The books fluttered down from the shelves like a flock of birds and disappeared into the box. When the bookcase was empty, Harry closed the lid.

'Epic!' cried Jack.

Harry tucked the box into his pocket and picked up the crystal trumpet. The vulture hopped from his shoulder and perched on the golden stand.

'That's right, my pet,' he said, offering the bird a hazelnut. 'You stay here and look after the castle while I'm gone.'

He faced Louisa and Jack. For the first time, he smiled. 'Let's go to the village!'

Chapter 14
Silver Notes

'Follow me,' said Harry. He led them through a small door at the side of the hall. They stepped onto a balcony overlooking the mountainside.

'Wow, you can see for miles!' exclaimed Louisa.

Jack gripped the iron rail. 'It's too high for my liking,' he said.

'We're about to go even higher!' grinned Harry. He clutched one of the diamonds hanging around his neck.

'Why do you hold different snowflakes each time you do magic?' asked Louisa.

'Each snowflake has a different power,' he said. His eyes twinkled. 'Guess what this one can do?'

'I don't want to know,' cried Jack.

Harry chuckled. 'Let's fly!'

They began to rise.

'Yippee!' cried Louisa. She stretched out her arms and glided effortlessly through the cold air, twisting and looping. 'Come on, Jack. This is fun,' she cried, and grabbed his hand.

'Arghh!' he wailed, as she whisked him up through the clouds, spiralling together.

Harry chuckled as they swooped to his side. 'Now you two have had some practice, let's head for the village.'

'What about Daisy, our horse?' asked

Louisa, pointing below to where Daisy stood, staring back up at them.

'She can come too!' laughed Harry, beckoning towards her.

In moments, the astonished horse was flying beside them. She snorted and pawed the air with her hooves.

'It's okay, Daisy,' Louisa reassured. 'You'll be home soon.'

'This way!' cried Harry, and flew ahead of them.

This is better than any dream, thought Louisa as they raced over tree-tops.

When they approached the village, Harry gave Jack the crystal trumpet. 'Blow into it. Go on!'

Jack grinned and blew into the glittering instrument. Without a sound, sliver notes poured from the trumpet.

A group of children were sledging below. As the notes fell on them, they looked up.

'It's Jack and Louisa!' they cried, pointing and waving. 'Our voices! We can talk!'

'We've got our voices back! Thank you!'

'You're welcome,' cried Jack, waving.

'Harry, isn't that wonderful?' said Louisa.

Harry looked thoughtful.

'Look, there's Daisy's owner!' Louisa cried. She pointed at a rosy-cheeked man who was gaping up at them in disbelief.

'Down you go, Daisy,' said Harry.

Daisy whinnied as she drifted towards the ground.

'Goodbye, Daisy,' called Louisa, fighting back the tears.

'Don't be sad,' called Jack. 'She's back where she belongs.'

'I know but I miss her already! I wish I could see her again!'

As they flew over the roof-tops, silver notes continued to flow towards the villagers' homes. Excited cries rang out as the villagers received their voices. 'I can talk!'

'I've got my voice back! I can sing!'

'Look, it's Jack and Louisa!'

'Who's with them? Is it the Miser?'

'It looks like him! Why has he come?'

They neared the village square and saw people pointing at Harry. As they landed beside the fountain, the villagers scattered and hid in their homes. They peeped through their windows but no one dared to venture out.

Louisa turned to Harry. 'They're still afraid of you,' she said.

Jack ran to each home, knocking on the doors. 'Come out. It's safe!'

The villagers peered around their doors. Gradually, they stepped into the square.

Louisa spoke to Harry, 'Stand on this ledge then everyone can hear you.'

'I d-don't know w-what to say,' he panicked, as a large crowd gathered.

Louisa squeezed his hand. 'Just tell them you're sorry. Imagine that you're talking to

Ice-Claw! You'll be fine.'

He cleared his throat. 'H-hello everyone. I'd like to say... how sorry I am... for stealing your voices and music. I've been... very selfish and foolish. It was wrong of me. I realise that I've made you all miserable. Can you forgive me? I'd like to be your friend.'

The crowd muttered, 'Friend? Him?'

'Does he mean it?'

'Can we believe him?'

Louisa nudged him, 'What about the books?'

'I want to return something else that belongs to you,' said Harry. He took out the gold box and opened the lid. As he did, out flew the books.

'Wow!' gasped the crowd, as they watched their books flutter back to their homes.

'I know I've spoilt your preparations for the Music Festival. To prove I'm sorry, I'd like to help you make the event happen. I hope you will share your music with me?'

The villagers looked doubtful, 'Is it a trick? Can we trust him?' they murmured.

Louisa stepped up, 'Don't be afraid. He's truly sorry and wants to help you!'

Suddenly, a familiar voice called out from the back of the crowd, 'We accept!'

The villagers' mood changed. Suspicious whispers became excited chatter. Louisa strained to see who had spoken. Amidst the bobbing heads, she saw that it George! She pushed through the crowd to meet him.

'George!' she called.

'My dear girl. You did it!' He gave her an affectionate hug.

'We couldn't have managed without the diamond snowflake,' she said, quietly and slipped the gem into his hand. 'Also, we've brought someone who wants to see you.'

Just then, Harry emerged from the crowd. 'Hello, George,' he said, in a solemn voice.

George stared at the cloaked figure in bewilderment. 'Harry? My…brother? Is it you?'

Harry hung his head in shame. 'Yes. It's me.'

George's face brightened. He flung his arms around his brother. 'I never expected to see you again!' he exclaimed. 'You went missing years ago! We searched and searched for you. There was a terrible avalanche. We assumed that you'd died. I gave up hope of ever finding you. I had no idea that you were The Miser!'

'It's my fault. I hid. I was ashamed of stealing from you and was too selfish to return the snowflakes. Besides, I liked staying far away from the village so that no one could tease me.'

'Harry?' questioned the old man with the white beard and curly moustache. He pressed through the crowd and joined them. For a moment he stared at Harry as if trying to recall a face long forgotten. 'I remember you when we were children. Everyone used to call you names because you stuttered. I'd forgotten about that. Is that what drove you to steal our voices?'

The crowd became quiet and listened intently. Harry nodded.

'I didn't realise how much we upset you! We're partly to blame for what has happened.'

The crowd nodded in agreement.

'Please accept my apology on behalf of everyone.'

'Here, here!' the villagers called.

The man offered his broad hand for Harry to shake. Harry smiled and shook the gentleman's hand with enthusiasm.

'Come on,' called the violinist. 'Let's get ready for the festival!'

'Yes!' Harry beamed. 'Just tell me what you need!'

Chapter 15
More Surprises

'We hold the festival in The Great Hall,' said the choirboy. 'Follow me.'

Everyone chattered with excitement as they followed the choirboy and Harry. As they approached the huge, double doors, Harry nodded. The doors swung open. The crowd gaped in awe.

'We usually hang lanterns around the hall,' said the choirboy.

Harry clicked his fingers. In seconds, colourful lanterns decorated the vast room.

'Wow!' the crowd marvelled.

'We need a stage over there. A space for dancing. Seats here,' directed the violinist.

Harry raised his staff. Louisa noticed that he kept one hand on his chest, *of course, he has to hold the snowflakes,* she thought. As he did, a wooden stage appeared. The villagers clapped with delight.

A little boy tugged Harry's robe, 'We need lots of cake, please, Sir!'

Harry chuckled.

'He looks as though he is enjoying himself,' Louisa whispered to Jack.

Harry continued to talk with the violinist and amaze the villagers with his magic until everything was ready for the festival.

Just then, Louisa spied the little girl who had lent her the pale, blue cloak. Her tummy tightened into a knot as she pictured the spoilt cloak left beside the castle moat. *I must explain to her*, she thought. She squeezed through the crowd.

'Hello,' she said, nervously.

'Louisa! I'm so excited that you've got our voices back!' the little girl cried.

'Me too! But I'm afraid your cloak is ruined. I fell through some ice and…'

'Oh! That's alright. You were very brave to face The Miser. I'm so happy! I can sing again! Thank you!'

Louisa smiled as the little girl wrapped her thin arms around her.

'I'd better change into my special dress. The festival is about to begin. Goodbye,' she called and skipped away.

'What a relief!' Louisa sighed.

'Come on,' said Jack, heading towards the buffet. 'Let's get some food!'

'Typical!' she laughed. She was about to follow when George called after them.

'Jack, we need you to place the crystal trumpet back on its stand ready for the grand opening.'

Jack's cheeks reddened. He glanced at the glittering trumpet in his hands. 'Oh! Err. Yes. I'd forgotten I was still holding it!'

George shuffled onto the stage and motioned for everyone to be quiet. They all watched as Jack carefully placed the trumpet on its elegant stone stand.

'Bravo!' the villagers applauded. 'Three cheers for Jack and Louisa! Hip hip hooray..!'

Louisa felt so proud that she thought her chest would burst.

'I said we could do this!' grinned Jack.

'Do you think the snow globe will send us back to Grandma's house soon?'

Jack was about to reply, when Harry joined them.

'Before the festival begins, I want to thank you for all you've done,' he said.

'Yes! Thank you for reuniting me with my brother,' cried George, slapping Harry on the back.

'You can tell you're brothers!' said Louisa, comparing their creased smiles and sparkling grey eyes.

'I suppose there is a resemblance,' laughed George. 'You look much better without your black hood.'

'I don't need to hide anymore,' replied Harry. I don't deserve your kindness after the way I've treated you.'

'Nonsense! It's all in the past,' cried George.

Louisa motioned to George and Harry to move closer. 'Will you tell everyone about the snowflakes?' she asked, in a hushed voice.

George and Harry exchanged a wary glance.

'Not yet,' said George. 'If the snowflakes can cause so much trouble between two brothers, imagine the chaos they would create in a whole village!' He stepped back and spoke to Harry, 'Now, I can't call you "The Miser" anymore.'

'Harry, will do nicely,' his brother replied, grinning.

Louisa turned to Jack. 'They're going to be great friends,' she remarked.

Before Jack could answer, the wind howled outside. It rattled the windows and rose in a crescendo above the chattering voices. Louisa spun round as the doors blew open and banged against the walls. The crowd gasped as a flurry of snow swirled into the hall.

'Look outside!' cried a little boy. 'The fountain! It's glowing!'

Louisa turned to Jack, 'The snow globe must be ready to send us back to Grandma's house! Come on!'

Louisa raced out of the hall into the whirling snow. The icy wind choked her breath. Across the square, the fountain radiated the same dazzling light that she had seen before.

'Wait for me!' cried Jack.

'Hurry!' she yelled.

Together they fought against the blizzard until they reached the fountain. They climbed onto the steps and looked back at the Great Hall. Through the driving snow, the figures of Harry and George were just visible, standing in the doorway, waving.

'Goodbye!' Louisa shouted, waving madly. The spiralling wind lifted them from the fountain. 'Not this again!' she wailed.

They were spun round until they could longer see the village. Just when Louisa had lost all sense of which way was up or down, the wind stopped. Thump! They dropped to the floor in Grandma's lounge, landing in a heap of snow!

'We're back!' exclaimed Louisa, grateful to be in the familiar room. 'The snow globe!' she cried, staring at the dome lying in her hands. A cheerful melody filled the room. Louisa beamed at Jack, 'The music's working!' she cried.

Just then, Grandma entered the room, 'Jack? Louisa? You're back!' she exclaimed. 'Oh, no! Not more snow! I've just finished clearing up the last lot!'

'We're really sorry, Grandma,' said Jack.

Grandma's attention was drawn from the snow that covered her carpet to the musical snow globe in Louisa's hands. 'My snow globe? You've mended the music box! How wonderful! I thought it was broken forever!'

'We're sorry about the snow,' said Louisa.

'Yes, it's a bit hard to explain,' added Jack.

'You don't need to explain,' Grandma replied. Her eyes shone brightly as she knelt beside them in the snow. To Louisa's amazement, she leant forwards and whispered, 'You're not the first to experience the magic of the snow globe!' and winked.

Acknowledgements

Firstly, a huge thank you to my amazing Mum and Dad for your incredible support. A special thank you to Mum, who was the catalyst for my writing journey!

My warmest thanks to my tutor and editor, Barbara Large, for your expertise.

Thank you to my fantastic illustrator, Dawn Larder, for your enthusiasm and stunning artwork.

Thank you to Quob Stables for allowing me to use their horse, Daisy, as a character in this book.

Heartfelt thanks to my friend, Elbrie dK, who was with me every step of the way!

Thank you to my brilliant, early readers, Sophie K, Helen K, Daniel dK, Jake dK, and Vicky W. It was a pleasure to share this story with you. Your feedback was invaluable!

Finally, thank you to my wonderful husband, Wai, for not allowing me to give up!

Daisy

Daisy is a 15.3hh Irish Draught/ Thoroughbred mare. She was born in 2007.

She loves to jump, especially when hunting or being ridden cross-country when she can really kick up heels and run. Her jump is bold and scopey but watch out, she's fast!

She has lovely paces on the flat. She is clever and tries hard to please. Just remember to ask her politely! When relaxing, Daisy enjoys, lying down, being groomed and given a gentle scratch behind the ears. She can be strong willed but is also very kind. Her home is Quob Stables, where she is loved by all!

About the Author

Anne grew up on a farm in Northamptonshire and dreamt of becoming a show jumper. Her parents sighed with relief when she chose the sensible option and became a primary teacher!

She began writing picture book stories in 2012, inspired by the antics of her three boys. She went on to study creative writing with Barbara Large.

Secrets of the Snow Globe — Vanishing Voices, is her first publication. It is the beginning of the *Secrets of the Snow Globe* series.

Find out more at www.anne-wan.com